THE PAJAMA ELVES

BY

HAYDEN EDWARDS

For my special elves

who always look dashing

on Christmas morning.

URGENT DELIVERY

 PAJAMA ELVES MAIL

TO: _____

_____

_____

_____

There are elves at the

North Pole who do

more than make toys -

they sew special pajamas

for good girls and boys.

SNUG-AS-A-BUG THREAD CO.
Dreamy Sleep Guarantee
SNUG-AS-A-BUG THREAD CO.
Dreamy Sleep Guarantee

Pajamas that are stitched

with a magical thread,

one that promises children

will sleep snug in their bed.

This special elf magic comes

with the guarantee,

that Santa can visit and

little ones will not see.

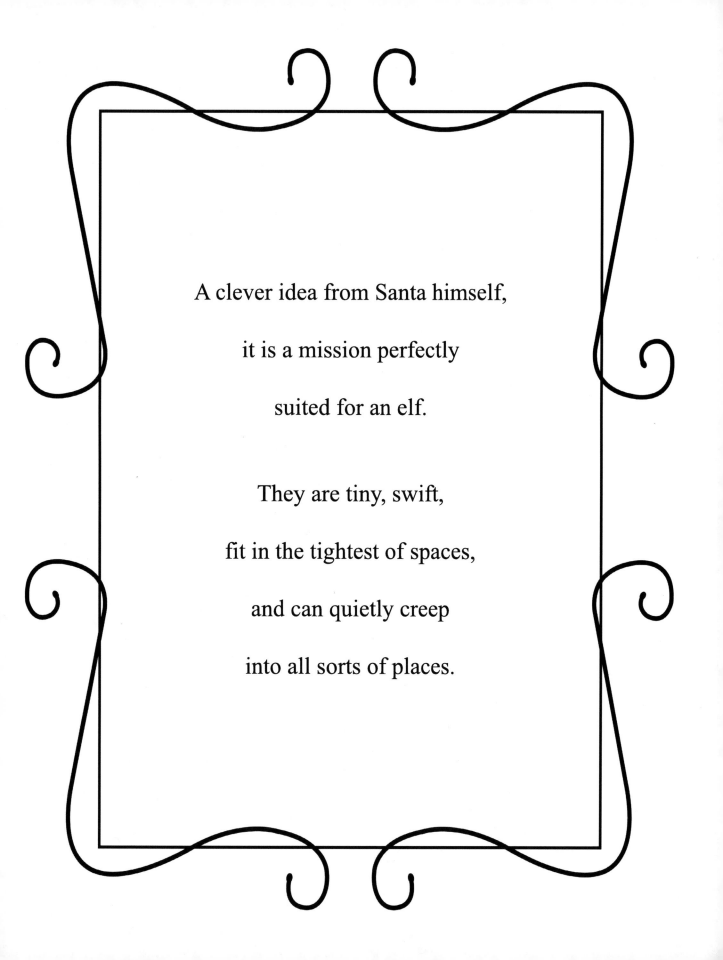

A clever idea from Santa himself,

it is a mission perfectly

suited for an elf.

They are tiny, swift,

fit in the tightest of spaces,

and can quietly creep

into all sorts of places.

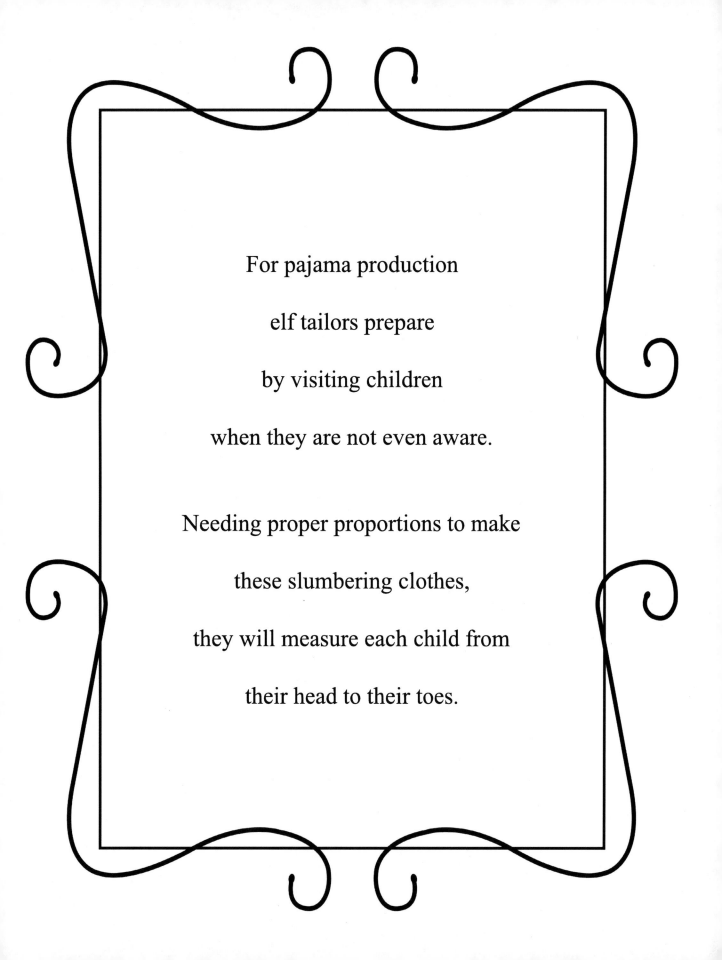

For pajama production

elf tailors prepare

by visiting children

when they are not even aware.

Needing proper proportions to make

these slumbering clothes,

they will measure each child from

their head to their toes.

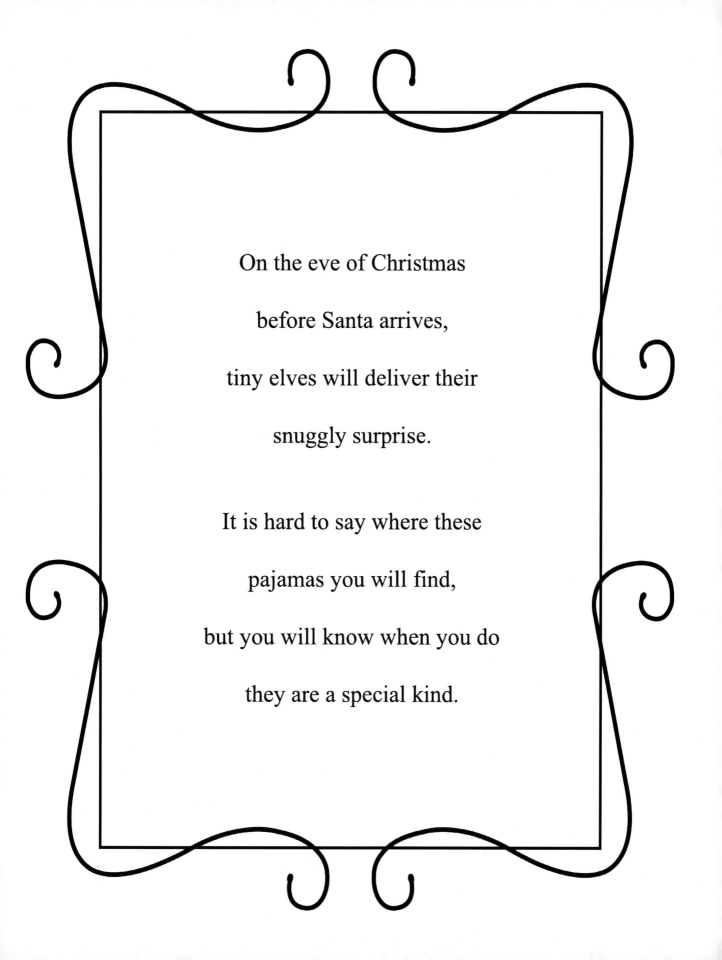

On the eve of Christmas

before Santa arrives,

tiny elves will deliver their

snuggly surprise.

It is hard to say where these

pajamas you will find,

but you will know when you do

they are a special kind.

They may ring your bell

or give your door a few knocks,

when you open it up

you may find a box.

Labeled "Urgent Delivery" -

remove the contents quick,

put on your new pajamas

and prepare for St. Nick.

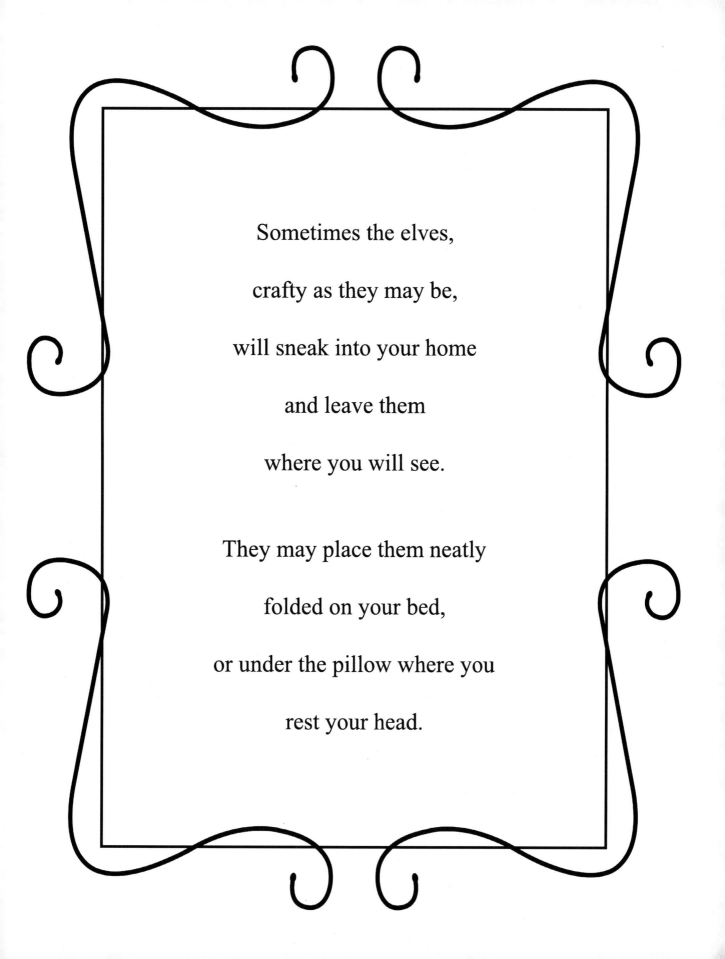

Sometimes the elves,

crafty as they may be,

will sneak into your home

and leave them

where you will see.

They may place them neatly

folded on your bed,

or under the pillow where you

rest your head.

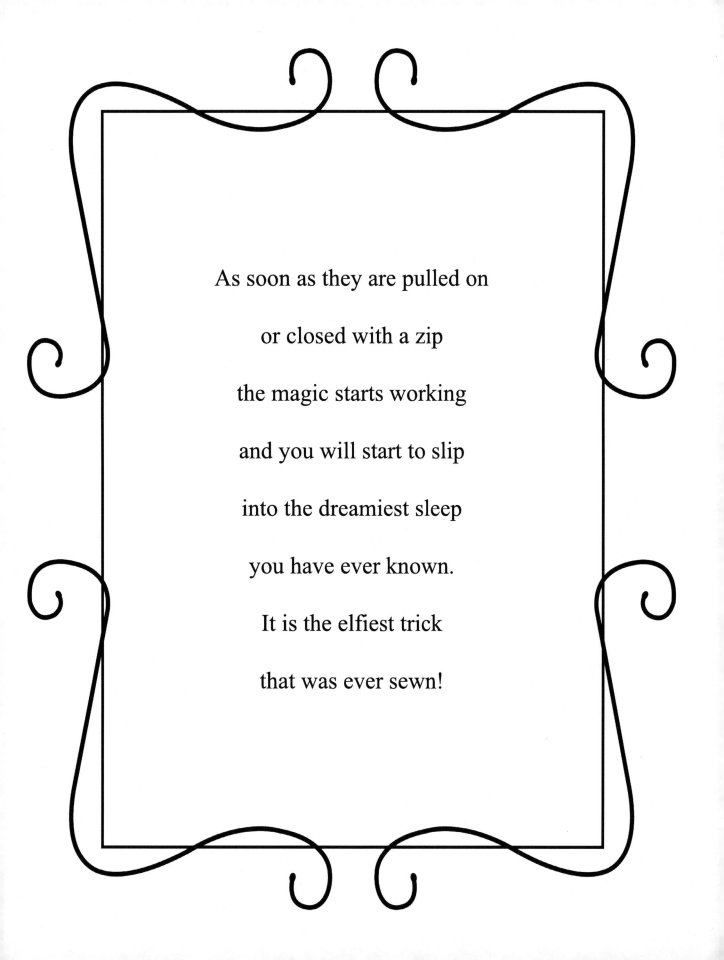

As soon as they are pulled on

or closed with a zip

the magic starts working

and you will start to slip

into the dreamiest sleep

you have ever known.

It is the elfiest trick

that was ever sewn!

So, this Christmas if there is a

question of how good you have been,

you will know Christmas Eve by the

pajamas you are in!

MERRY CHRISTMAS

Made in United States
North Haven, CT
03 December 2021